Sweetheart, Baby, Darling

Sweetheart, Baby, Darling

Poems by Philip Memmer

Word Press

For Joan,
with thanks and
all best wishes,
Phil
4/8/09

Published by Word Press
P.O. Box 541106
Cincinnati, OH 45254-1106

Typeset in Lucida Grande and Palatino by WordTech Communications LLC, Cincinnati, OH

ISBN: 1932339310
LCCN: 2003113603

Poetry Editor: Kevin Walzer
Business Editor: Lori Jareo

Visit us on the web at www.word-press.com

Cover art: "Sleeping Poet" by DeLoss McGraw, courtesy of the artist

Author photograph: Della Nohl

For Michelle, my sweetheart,

for Henry Owen, my baby,

and for Deena, my darling.

ACKNOWLEDGMENTS

Thanks are due to the following publications and their editors for first printing poems from this book:

Calapooya	"Seven A.M."
The Chattahoochee Review	"Bedroom"
Cider Press Review	"Real-Life Encounters With Angels"
Clackamas Literary Review	"The Firekeepers"
Connecticut Review	"Consignment Lingerie"
Folio	"In Reverse"
Free Lunch	"Winter Window"
Kestrel	"Sweetheart, Baby, Darling" "The Language of Sorrow"
Lullwater Review	"Buy Fruit," "Lost," "To the Next Renters," "Two Half-Poems,"
Mid-American Review	"Cups"
Northeast Corridor	"Stretching"
Pinyon Poetry	"Colorado"
Poems & Plays	"The Wife Test"
Poetry	"Letter to a Friend," "Tabletop World"
Poetry Daily	"Tabletop World"
Poetry Northwest	"Garden," "Haunted Mini-Golf," "Peace," "Today, the Houses," "The Weather Where You Are"
Puerto del Sol	"What He'll Do If She Leaves"

Southern Poetry Review	"Details," "Noise," "Three Poems for Point Breeze"
Underwood Review	"Sidewalk Penny," "The Triphibian Atomicar"

"Love" was originally printed in *Seven Hundred Kisses,* an anthology from *Yellow Silk* magazine (HarperSanFrancisco, 1997).

"What He'll Do If She Leaves" and "To the Next Renters" appeared in *Proposing From the Brooklyn Bridge* (Grayson Books, 2003).

"The Apartment" was published as a chapbook by piccadilly press (2001).

Several other poems from this collection were published in "For Resident," a chapbook from FootHills Publishing (2002).

"The Wife Test" is for Thom Ward.

"The Language of Sorrow" is for Sean Thomas Dougherty.

CONTENTS

THE LANGUAGE OF SORROW

Acquaint yourself first with its alphabet—
the usual twenty-six letters

and countless others—the characters
between the characters, always silent,

shaped like faces, dark houses, fruit.
Next, the words. Familiar, yes,

but you must learn each
again, with new meanings. Snow:

a form, often brief, of comfort.
Peach: *flavor of remembered joy.*

Can you be taught? Maybe.
But the only course is by correspondence,

and who would answer such letters?
There is no six-cassette set,

no *Dick & Jane*, no *Strunk & White*—
there is no grammar. Some are fluent,

but in places where Sorrow is spoken
there are no native speakers

save the stutterers—masters
of their language's cadence—

and those eloquent others who talk
in their sleep, but sleep alone.

I.

For Resident

TABLETOP WORLD

Blasting a note to the crisp flags of Main,
the toy train hisses through fields of felt,
then over a painted stream by way

of an intricate matchstick bridge.
It passes the mill, the painted toy men
posed in their toil near the mine's closed mouth,

and curves through hills, the pinecone forest
crowded with horses and soldiers.
And now as the engine dips into the tunnel

the fluorescent sun goes dark with a click,
the song begins at Ye Olde Saloon,
and the rows of streetlamps snap on.

If by day you shoveled coal, you shovel now by night.
If you washed clothes, you wash clothes.
If you had no legs and sat alone

in your chair by the glassless window
you sit there now, and wait for the sun
to flicker back, for the looped tune to stop

as the engine zips through the station on Main
and the boy in the boxcar waves—
his motorized arm like a metronome,

his hair blown wild by an unseen wind,
his mouth a silently shouting O
as he tries to skip town yet again.

SEVEN A.M.

after Hopper

If you want a reason to stop
there's not one here. The clock

is stalled, the bookshelf
is bare, the window's been left

with only three bottles,
two prints. *No Sale,*

the register almost whispers.
Though the storefront is lit

like a church, this isn't light
you can rest in. No doubt

the door is locked. The owner
twisted the key, slipped it

to the floor of his long pocket,
walked the three small steps

and turned to the woods—
as you yourself now turn,

following the narrow path
where you'll never find him.

THREE POEMS FOR POINT BREEZE

I.

February. The barber curses
his furnace, his text for night school,

the cars lined up the block for inspection,
their coughs and hisses, scrapes and dents.

He sweeps my hair into the morning's pile.
Outside, the scrape of a metal shovel,

the grocer's stockboy clearing the alley,
pounding ice from the bent downspout.

When the doorbell rings, it's the Witnesses.
When the mail comes, it's for RESIDENT.

II.

Closing, the grocer calls *neighbor*
because he can't remember my name—

he's Bob or Rob, or Ron. His mother
naps by the candy, forgets

the days of the week. Eighteen months
I've lived on this street, Saturdays fading

like soul from a passing car
into the skyline and river, the exhaust

of the leaving-for-good—
I still don't know where North is.

III.

Street empty. A warm day ends
with sore-throat wind, chimes

from the next yard. Their Dalmatian
sniffs at the chain-link fence, cocks her head

to the school lot's dark, the slow clock
of basketball, backboard, blacktop.

In the glow of their draped windows
shadows walk, wave their arms—

unshaped, unaged, unsexed,
numbers on doors, numbers on mailboxes.

LETTER TO A FRIEND

Two weeks waiting for the pepper seeds you sent
to sprout in the window-sill planter: it's this new place,
new windows. The angles of light aren't sharp enough
to come in, to bring up shoots.

And no, I haven't been to the shore yet. Inexcusable,
it is so near. But as Du Fu says, *In this secluded life*
I move toward truly feeling. I leave the windows open
some nights, and wake up in cool, dry sheets.

And if the coolness carries into the soil, so what?
The windows open out and the rain runs straight
down the tilted glass. Its noteless music
pleases me, though the peppers remain uncharmed.

A woman just went past the window
with her baby, who was good and not crying.
If she had been, I would have comforted her with a gift
of peppers, assuming any had grown. None have.

Perhaps the seeds have a point, making me wait.
Even I enjoy staying in all day, watching or not
watching the people that go by, going out late
afternoons to the mailbox, to see what has come to me.

MAGIC HOUR

. . .that time of day around twilight or dawn when colors seem iridescent and the world of objects magical.
—Dave Viera,
Lighting for Film and Electronic Cinematography

It's easy to picture myself in the frame
while the dust falls, articulated

by golden light from the west window.
I'd wait alone, a small triangular shadow

under my cheekbone, and pace, slowly,
the rusted steel of a fire escape

until the light decided for me—
make it up to her / let her go—

the sky's dazzle like rainbowed oil.
Then I'd walk all the places we walked,

silently weeping in silhouette,
the cuts so precisely timed

it's almost rhyme when the theme rises
and the landscape dissolves to her face.

Lucky for me there are engines, always
engines, speeding and stalling, breaking

the spell of the light. And it's a little late,
almost sunset—no time

even to wish, as the clouds shift,
that I'd handled the whole thing better.

Lucky for me darkness comes on
before the streetlamps—just a bit—

and the heart's heroes and ingénues
fade in the hum of these local extras

who cross my street in the sudden night,
carrying home some bread or fruit,

their lines not heard, their scene not lit.

EVERY SUMMER,

this field by the highway
thickens with flowers—
but the trees stay bare,

black as if burned
or soaked with rain,
their dark made darker

by the tangled way
they wait, shadeless,
in the vagrant wind.

If you're the one
who wants to heal
everyone's hearts,

pull to the shoulder.
Jump the wire and run
to the land's wound, the trees

like stitches, rough
and sure to scar.
If you're the one,

scare the crows
from their low branch.
Tear out the lace of vines,

the abandoned nests
with their egg-shards
and gray down—

imagine the field
in unbroken bloom
and save us all.

I'm not stopping.
I'm letting hills in the rear-view
bury the grove

as dusk's exhaust
stalls everywhere.
I'm weaving, passing,

eyeing the dash.
As a thousand miles
roll the nines to zeroes,

I'm singing to no one.

NIGHT MUSIC

My footsteps echo
    off stoops and false-fronts.

Straying from wires
    and night-lit cloud,

an alley's breeze
    slips in beneath my coat.

Who wrote the words
    to this tune I'm humming,

all *sha* and *la*
    and a girl's name crackling

from the shifting address
    of a memory's station?

As my paces fade
    in the crossroads' quiet,

I can almost hear it
    sift through the fences

like the falling riff
    of a far-off train,

its transient's secret sleep
    my restless freight.

II.

Apartment

BEDROOM

The green-painted bureau, the bottom drawer
halfway out, her leggings and slips
spilling over. On the pillow, the man's silk robe.
On the floor, the purple blanket and top-sheet
pulled off the bed. *Fucking or fighting,*
we'd say, as if love were doomed
to extremes, as if devotion had nothing to do
with the laziness of sunlight moving
over blue carpet, the small space where they dress,
the closet they share. There's a feeling here—
late summer lacing the clutter, the trees
tossing the afternoon through the window—
if the lovers who live here were lucky enough
to be home, together, maybe they *would* be
making love—in this light, they'd move
slowly, leave the curtains open to feel
the rays like hands, to see each other
until their eyes squeezed shut—
but she's out. Buying groceries, stuff for the house.
He's home by himself, daydreaming away
this morning's argument, remaking the bed
and putting some small things back in place.
When she comes home, they'll collapse together
the way they'd let go of a long held breath,

not kissing yet, not clutching, just feeling
their weight in that room, the messy lushness
that is their one luxury.

DETAILS

Homemade bread flavored with cheddar
browns in the oven. When it's half done
he lays a glaze of butter, reverses the trays
so the loaves color evenly. He knows the way
the dog moves when the car is close
to home, the tone the finished bread makes
tapped with a spoon. When she walks in,
the étouffée steams on a bed
of rice, the bread is sliced and piled thick
under a cloth napkin. Her surprised smile,
the favorite wine, his lips brushing
her neck, the scar there from a childhood
scalding, a splash of boiling stove water.
When he enters her, her small bite of air.
His. His free hand moving over her
skin, afterwards, from knee to shoulder, his chest
against her spine the way she likes, his arms
tight, his body heavy and astounded.
Now she is thinking about her thirst,
thin and light in her throat, the cool glass
he'll bring to their bed when she asks.
At the refrigerator, his shiver, the metal
lid of the water bottle twisting, the laughter

of water into a cup, the floor squeak
as he turns from the counter. His breath calm
as he leans, touching the full glass to her chin.

NOISE

Their day is just starting. In the late-morning glare
they're rediscovering each other's faces. They don't know
it'll be days before they make love again,
or that when they do, they'll lose their rhythm
at every TV laugh-track through the wall—
it won't be like last night, that wildness.
The note is still taped to their unit door,
the sheet torn—SOME OF US LIKE TO SLEEP—
WE DON'T WANT TO LISTEN TO YOU FUCK.
They haven't found it, or thrown it out,
or dug it from the trash to re-read it.
He's remembering how their bellies met
with a slapping sound, a music
like shoes pacing the ceiling,
and he wants her again, hears the hum in her throat
as he pulls her closer, kisses her neck.
If only they could stay in bed all day.
But they can't—she has errands to run.
Later, she promises. She gets up to make coffee,
discovers they're almost out, marks her list—
at the store she'll meet a neighbor
and worry if he's staring, if she's blushing.
At the laundry room, at the wall of locked mailboxes
she'll think someone sees—what? Something
she'll work all day to scour, something

her husband won't touch her for fear of, lying awake
under another couple's fight.
But now he's dressing, their last kiss in his whistle,
and as she pours the coffee she listens,
remembers how she straddled his chest,
pulled his mouth to her thighs.
As he swings into the kitchen
the turtleneck he'll wear to hide the marks
still hangs in the bedroom closet.
And he's still whistling, bare-chested and warm
when he kisses her one more time
then opens the door.

IN REVERSE

Outside the rented hall, the guests are smashed,
leaning on a rail by the parking lot and waving
as the car, ringing with strung cans, arrives.
Out comes the groom in his tux, the bride

in her gown. Her girlfriends throw a bouquet
at her turned back—but this is her day,
single-handed she makes the catch. Inside,
a pianist plays show tunes, bottles fill

with champagne and light. Between chatter
and pictures, piece by piece, the guests build
the cake, perfect angel food and icing
the bride and groom seal shut with a knife.

How quickly everyone sobers. In the wedding garden,
uncles unfold chairs, people sit.
Someone puts the cake away, the music stops,
and in the flashbulb glare the couple walks

backward to the flowered trellis. It's a wonder
she doesn't trip over that gown. They kiss,
and gently, so gently, he veils her face.
They pull the rings from each others' fingers—

Do I, they say. The minister drones on
about forever. It feels like forever.
They don't hear a word. She's watching the breeze
shake a hair on his cheek. He can't believe

how beautiful she is, eyes full of tears
as her father leads her, by the arm, out of there.

GARDEN

She has a little space between the shingles
and the side fence, not enough

to lie down in, a closet of dirt and wood.
But what she plants there fades, eaten

to limp veils. She's been with him a year
in this town with too much rain

but no storms, nothing to shock her
awake at night. When she turns over,

he turns over, they go back to sleep,
the window behind their heads

opaque with moonlight.
She doesn't know what he'd do

if she were to shake him, tell him to dress
and walk to the end of the tree-dark street

with her, to the field empty of everything
but that moon, the stars she wishes

she knew. This morning they wake up
face to face, only knees touching,

her eyes to the wall, her back to the edge.

PEACE

The opposite, he thinks, of the garbage truck
grinding the block's excess,
or the city tractor serrating the yard
for a new length of pipe to the street.

But there's also a sort of comfortable faith
in dragging the can to the curb.
And the lawn torn up for his family's sake
is reassuring, in a way—

even his wife's chrysanthemums.
Ripped from her garden, they abide
in terra cotta planters. They survive,
though the pots he bought are cheap—

too heavy, no holes for water's escape.
He imagines the soil molding
beneath the stems, as she says it will—
maybe she's right, he'll kill them all,

each last hysterical blossom.
Out they'll go, two cans
choked with wilts and tight stems,
and when the workers are finally done

the yard will be smooth to the street—
no more ditches or diesels, no more
tape or blinking lights. Just a beach
of newly combed dirt. His wife sulking,

but not screaming. The waves of evening
traffic receding, towing his gaze
past the street lamp
to what was, in daylight, a horizon.

WHAT HE'LL DO IF SHE LEAVES

He thinks he'd start working out, though he wouldn't.
He thinks he'd travel, find someplace like a desert

just waiting for footprints—he'd walk for hours
then camp, watch the sun set over dunes

and never miss her, his fire's embers hissing
like an old horse's tail sifting the night

behind the farmhouse they rented one summer.
He'd have strength like that, the way he used to

when they ran on the beach, circling each other,
their tracks becoming braided and blurred,

and when he meets the new woman in the desert
they'll walk side by side, their prints distinct—

but first she'll appear on the horizon, a tiny dot.
Then he'll give her water, he'll show her everything

and they'll exit the desert, ready for a life
of love made in famous places with streetcars

or marinas or outdoor markets
where they won't be held together by fear—

if she stays, she stays because she wants him.
If she leaves, she leaves with a *film-noir* note,

a dark past and a broken promise to meet him
in Paris or Prague. Wearing his custom tux

he'll talk like Bogart, drink like Cotten,
lean on the white baby grand with a style

he can't manage now, still a little off-balance
as he waits in the room his wife stormed out of

hours ago. It was hours ago.

STRETCHING

She'd hardly made a sound
as she rolled her shoulders together, her spine
aching in the shape of an office chair.
Her husband's hand on her thigh startles,
sudden and not wanted, not
when today's her ninth day straight
at a job that pays no overtime, not
when she has to walk the quiet house,
dressing for no one to notice, eating
too fast, too early. His fingers move
and she knows from his touch how he sees her—
dazzling in first light, her arms rising, lifting
her ribs to her skin, her neck and hair
thrown back as if laughing—she knows
he mistook her sob for a sigh, woke up
to beauty and pain, saw only beauty,
and she hates that he doesn't understand,
that it's not sympathy as his fingers slide
to her waist, his thumb drawing empty circles.

When she weaves her fingers with his, it's harder work
than anything she'll do in her ten-hour shift.
When she lifts his hand to her chest, then higher,

it's harder than the whole day of cold-calling.
It's work holding his hand like that,
kissing their meshed knuckles. It's work.

LOST

I.

He finds himself in the shaky light
of new candles burned to stubs.
Had he felt her breath? Her hands on his back?
She's asleep now. In the other room,

the radio still plays to the empty glasses—
maybe it's the wine that makes things hazy.
What had they done to each other
to make such a tangle of sheets?

The shifting reds of the bedside clock
connect to tell him three hours have passed.
When did they light the candles?
Undress? Wander off into sleep?

II.

He hates being lost, takes steps to avoid it—
studying maps, highlighting routes,
driving in daylight when possible. Still,
there's construction and detours, the weather.

Once he was lost in the New York subway,
the schedule misread in suburban terror—
but at least there had been the schedule,
street numbers in tile on the walls.

For him, the worst part of being lost
comes later—his destination at last
reached by accident, in darkness,
both the right and the wrong routes forgotten.

III.

The minutes on the clock advance
between his blinks, it seems, and now
as she curls into him, sighing awake,
it's not the hours but the years he wants back—

all the places and promises
they've passed through half asleep
to arrive here, wherever here is.
It couldn't have just been the wine.

He listens to the random ticking of the pipes
until she sits up—*Even better*
than that time at the coast. He nods.
But east or west? Day or night?

III.

That All?

TODAY, THE HOUSES

are just houses, blue or white,
shuttered against the heat.

And the birds are birds. The crows
aren't wicked, the doves
aren't sad. Their songs are just

their songs. Their hearts,
for all their nervous speed,
are only hearts. Delicate—

with only your hand
you could crush them, your own heart
closed like a fist in your chest—

a grip that the light,
if it were more than light,
might reach through and open.

HAUNTED MINI-GOLF

a local Halloween attraction

The Devil's mouth is a tunnel,
cloven in three directions

through the rusting dark of his skull.
His teeth chew a creaking circle.

Even your daughter knows—
if you want a prize from the masked attendant,

you have to ring the bell
hung deep in the loops of this throat.

Finesse beat par in The Graveyard,
but putt too gently here

and your ball spits back down his tongue.
An inch to the right or left

and you drop from a pointed ear.
The eyes are crossed, the laugh is cheerless,

but it's Saturday night in America—
admit you want it, all of it,

the wind cool, the floodlights orange,
the wannabe Succubus selling Cokes—

and yes, that tinny electric ping
for the Ghost who tugs your coat,

the voice you love
turned sweet by greed

as the teenage werewolf looks up from his booth
and the forked tongue starts to sing.

"REAL-LIFE ENCOUNTERS WITH ANGELS"

There's *The Stranger,* trained in CPR,
who's gone when the half-drowned man is sure to live.

And the figure, a floating dress of light,
that leads the missing child home through the dark.

Angels, sent from Heaven to aide us,
the pamphlet at the check-out counter says—

there are angels in hospital hallways,
riding trains, pretending to read *The Herald*

but always watching, always ready
to catch a stroller, take a bullet, call police.

The nightshift clerk must read them all
as she struggles to stay awake—

which shabby nighthawk will be revealed
as *Her Real Father, Filthy Rich?*

In the warped eye of the corner mirror
anyone's sleeves could be wings,

but it's late, and out in the lot
my car breathes ghosts through the snow.

That all? she asks.
The lights hum over the rows.

And because tonight I'm only her only
customer, and not her *Miracle*

Midnight Mechanic—or even
her loyal Shepherd, three-legged and blind,

whining to wake her to fire—
my dimes shine down to her hand.

SIDEWALK PENNY

Prank or wish, it never fails
to catch my eye, stuck as it is
between the carved hearts and handprints,
pressed there, heads, when the walk was fresh.

Who counted its luck so little
to leave it here, just out of reach
to the stony fingers? And mine as well,
teased by its rain-buffed glare.

But better this than the block cracked,
the cement crumbled, the initials and loves
split by weeds, and the penny free
to be claimed, spent on a gumball or thought—

and so much better this than the mouth
of a restaurant register's cup,
have one, leave one, need one, take one,
one of a grimy, forgotten dozen.

I’d rather stop, and bend at the knees
for just a moment before I realize
the glow is the same glow as always—
nobody’s fortune, a fading face,

the good year rubbed away.

THE TRIPHIBIAN ATOMICAR

Who remembers now where Tom Swift went
in his Atomicar, or what it meant
to be triphibian?
                    I know I don't.
Maybe he traveled time. Or sped on land
in air and underwater. Or sped on land
in air and outer space.
                          Meanwhile, elsewhere,
Danny Dunn's marvelous homework machine
rattled with answers.
                          The Hardy Boys searched
for the crisscross shadow, the melting face.

All those secret hideouts and hidden stairways.
All those false floorboards,
                                those open graves
we fell into, the villain lurking above
with his wide shovel. And how many times
were we tied and blindfolded, gagged, out cold?
Such narrow escapes . . .
                          But none of it stopped us—

the antigravity, the antimatter—
we followed every tunnel,
hardly aware
of our goose-eggs, our arms in their white slings.

But when the doctor saws off the plaster cast
and fresh air, for the first time in weeks,
lifts the tiny hairs
how fragile
an arm becomes, moth-pale and flaking,
nothing but breakable
bone beneath the skin.
No more leaping from rocks, no more inventions—
the bedsheet parachutes
never opened,
and who needs a Secret Code anyway
when your left wrist aches a little in the rain?

We flipped our collars up with Judy Blume
and Hinton's denim heroes.
Happy sometimes,
sometimes drunk, our parents kissed and swore
between their silences.
How did we survive?
In Social Studies, we made relief maps
of starving nations.

In Art we clipped headlines,
used strips of Crime and Obituary
to papier mâché a laughing human face.

Enough to make you search for that Atomicar,
no matter what its fuel
or where it left you.
Or for Chet, the Hardy Boys' chubby sidekick,
who drove a jalopy.
Oh, that jalopy...
We speed away. The trunk is full of sandwiches
and antidotes and keys.
We'll know the villain
by his curled mustache. We'll solve the case
in time for supper. We'll only hurt a little,
a little,
and sleep all night like the dead.

CUPS

In one country, I read, mourners sprinkled tea
into each tomb, king or not.
                    I've forgotten why—
they'd kiss the earth, then scatter the leaves.

How could they drink without weeping?
Even so, tea was prized.
                              Here it's cheap,
it's nothing. I brew cup after cup, wait

for the leaves to leak through, for the dull scent
to pour over the mug's rim,
                              and watch the tree
by the window, a willow like any willow,

a wilt of green.
                    The tapwater's rusty.
I never knew I could be this tired.

CONSIGNMENT LINGERIE

Even beneath the humming lights
that make the coats look dirty,
the back aisle's wink of rhinestone and snap
defies the sign, *Last Chance.*

Not much sells—
everyone knows the least-used lace
is used. Once a week
the salesgirl dusts the shelf

where rising sun kimonos
settle, neatly creased,
their characters lost
in the folded dark's translation.

Still, the shoebox of garters
is nearly cheerful. The tarnished cart
with its snake's nest of straps
still promises dalliance,

and if you could gaze in her eyes
just once, the headless mannequin
in the velvet corset
might reach out her unpainted hand

and ask you to dance.

RUNE

I.

I take the leather sack and search,
as the party hostess instructs,
for the one tile that feels warm,
and open my palm to a blank.

Figures, I laugh, and reach to return it.
She stops me and smiles.
Over.
On the other side a single stroke,
straight and deep, painted black.

The winter of your spiritual life,
the companion pamphlet explains.
You will accomplish little of value
in this, a time of waiting.

II.

I believe in nothing just enough
to stay up all night wondering,
so I finish my drink and leave,
walk home through the falling snow.

Had the tile felt warm?
I imagine the hostess, her hand in the bag,
endowing her chilly favorite
with a pinch of extra heat.

But no, they'd all seemed cold.
And smooth—as if the marks came later,
after I'd chosen, impossibly burned
by some unfathomed power in my grasp.

III.

My rune involves no left, no right,
and thus no chance of reversal—
however I happened to choose this mark,
there's just one possible meaning.

When I turn the corner, four young deer
step without fear by the streetlamp.
That means something to someone, I'm sure—
if not their mere presence, the tracks.

It's lucky even to see a deer
so soon past the close of the season—
four at once in the unbroken snow
is enough of a vision for me.

The winter of my spiritual life . . .
They vanish, as deer do, in the trees.
As their white tails fade, I keep walking.
What more, in this time, need I wait for?

SWEETHEART, BABY, DARLING

I'm behind the county road-kill truck
again, nowhere to look for miles

but straight in its full bed.
Where does it go? What field or pit or fire

do we tend for the deer
and raccoons, the smashed-beyond-telling?

The closest, a doe, rests her chin
on the very edge of the bed—

no, she's dead, she's not resting,
though back at the house my oldest dog

could be sleeping this way, her neck
at a slightly more natural angle, and my wife

could be there beside her, cooing
sweetheart, baby, darling, this bed

is broken, there's too much gravity
for just one dog. With each bump,

the deer seems to startle, then ease.
Gravity—we want the earth, and the earth

wants us, even the good ground
of the mattress, the loud ground

of the truck bed. The men in the cab
are talking, lifting coffee

in styrofoam cups. Every day
they do this. As the passenger gestures,

I pretend he's telling the story
of his hatred for the county's tools—

the pitchfork and shovel, the gloves
and the weighty boots—how he spites them,

lifts each of the shattered in his arms,
then goes on living. I pretend

he knows how to do that, he's known
for years. All I need to do

is follow close, hold my breath, and overhear.

IV.

What Seemed Like Mountains

COLORADO

I never thought they weren't ours, those places
where we snapped pictures through the windshield
two weeks into our marriage, guardrails hazy with speed.
It didn't matter that what seemed like mountains changed
in the vanishing point, turned to storm clouds
to heat-shimmer to nothing. It didn't matter
that the road was older than we were, cracked
by thousands of cars, or that each pull-off
had two cans for fast-food trash from Denver.
Our photos are all depth, the distance clear
and waiting behind the unfocused foreground
as if we'd planned to show the way we dreamed.
It never mattered to me that we stood on asphalt,
though now I'd see the bottle-glass and ash
and doubt the permanence of anything.
We looked beyond the highway's painted lines,
her hand just under my shirt at the waist—
that mattered, and the sun setting on snow-caps.
Not the sick pines rowed behind us, or our thinning shadows.
Not whatever it was the radio had been playing,
some pop-song about the end of the world.

THE FIREKEEPERS

Beneath a roaring, painted fire
reduced by wind to embers,
an arrow of peeling flame

points off the highway to nothing
but a ragged patch of brush—
a campsite, once, or a small motel,

the kind of place you stop at
when you catch yourself snapping
awake, driving late and long

and alone. But now it's afternoon.
It's been years since anyone slept here.
The sun is dazzling, the traffic is heavy,

and as I pass the failing billboard
I exactly know the minutes
to reach my lover's drive.

Last week, the porch light was off,
the door was locked, and fumbling there
for the window box key, I could imagine

the house vacant—then lit again,
by other lives. The two of us
emptied out, buried or burned,

the awkward man with his hand at the bell
just a salesman, or the landlord.
Nobody likely to stay.

The next sign says I've arrived
in the Endless Mountains Region—
six exits, miles I can count,

nothing endless about it
but the feeling—the mild greens
unchanging, the highway

rising and falling, the radio
coming in, going out. A torch song
from another time, her favorite—

but a new version, without the heart.

THE WEATHER WHERE YOU ARE

Cold, the paper says. Our yard must be frozen.

But clear, too,
so maybe you've taken that star book
and walked out, shivering, to learn a new constellation.

Pegasus, maybe.
There must be wind,
as there is here, to make the pages flutter,

and I'm sure the dog goes with you,
a little nervous
if your mood is quiet.

Enough moonlight, and her stare is an amber void.

But I hope she's there at your side,
as I should be,
and stretching that perfect dog-stretch.

I hope, when you point and gasp,
                    she follows the line
you trace from mouth to wing—

the form, together, we found so hard to find.

YOUR WEEK AWAY ON BUSINESS

I lie on your side of the bed, pick up your book,
its torn cover throbbing with lovers.
Mouth to Source, their Passion is the River . . .

Through my face reflected in the window,
I watch our world—in one eye the sunset, in the other
the mailbox, the maple thick in my throat.

And along my chest, the roadside ditch
with its stream of rain, the lovers' names
in glossy backwards script.

Their river roils, purple with sighs.
It's only Tuesday. One by one in the dark
the cars course like hands through my body.

TWO HALF-POEMS

Before you, I'd go to the jetty's edge
alone. I'd drive the hardest curving roads
through the smallest towns, the gray lanes turning
out of the trees to gray sky and gray water
and the black plank of rock. I'd walk to the edge,
listening to the gulls' hunger—I knew where
to use my loneliness. The dark crevices filled
with spray, then drained.

The hot bath a failure,
you step from the tub, angrier now than you were
when you got home from job-hunting, sore,
your feet heavy. You don't want me to touch you
and there's nothing I can say. I hand you a towel,
you rub your steaming skin red. The pipes sweat
with the water that burns through the house.

"BUY FRUIT"

Four in the morning.
I've woken her, dressing
for work. *Fruit,*

buy fruit, she says,
and she's back to sleep.
For now, the murmur

is all I have of her—
a hunger for orange,
a crisp bouquet

of apples. The stand
where I'll fill a sack
with bananas, the star fruit

she loves for its shape.
She goes to work,
to class, comes home

when I'm in bed.
Rinsed, arranged,
the fruit waits

for her keys’ rattle,
the wash of moon
through the open door,

her hand, tired,
reaching for a dream’s
true skin.

WINTER WINDOW

We want to wake up to snow—

the world blank and brilliant,
shocking with purity,

as if with the lights out
we'd dreamt through all of December

to a place of just brightness and ourselves.
The time glows across the room—

it's dark, late, that hour
when each thinks the other sleeps

and neither of us risks asking.
Will we be disappointed?

If I raise the blinds to let the moon in,
we'll see each other

dreaming of the thing we want.

TO THE NEXT RENTERS, WHO DRIVE BY FOR THE SECOND TIME AS WE PACK TO LEAVE OUR FIRST APARTMENT

If you've ever left a place you loved
you know how we've spent the day imagining
your little crimes, how you'll hang
your awful painting where the clock should be
and never see the mistake.
You know how we'll stop, as you do now,
at the corner's red signal—
how we'll see your plants in our windows
and almost feel the angle of light
falling on your unmade bed.

Be patient with us. For once,
I barely notice the sticking drawers
or the floor's squeak spot echoing
as we drag furniture from the bedroom.
For once, my wife doesn't complain
how the radiator won't keep us warm—
you must be able to see her
prying out nails with a hammer,
each picture-frame leaving a clean square
we'll mean nothing to.

Give us a few minutes more
to belong here, to remember
how we unpacked the new dishes
and cooked our first dinner in this kitchen,
how we let the stereo blast as we kissed
once in each room.
Let us rest between trips to the car,
sit by this monument of boxes
and remember the spider's eggs in the hamper,
or how we burned a hole in the kitchen counter
with a pan still hot from the stove.
Give us time to re-check the rooms.
Let us stay until we're sure
we've forgotten nothing.

THE WIFE TEST

You merely wanted to stop the world
with a handful of clever words,
but only three lines in

you know you've lost her,
her eyes already beginning to wander
the room and its waiting chores—

laundry and dusting, the 1040 form—
tedious all, but not so tedious
as the first sentence of your latest poem.

Neither of you wants to hear the rest.
The critique, though silent, is finished.
But she asked you to read it aloud,

even she'll admit it, and now
there are only a few lines left—
lines you can see as you speak them

halt, sputter, as if from the start
they embarrassed you—
before she heard them, before

you even wrote them. She smiles
and leaves you with them.
They are more yours now than she is.

LOVE

All night we hadn't slept, expecting
something more. What were we missing there?
The sheets tangled under our bodies

like a Rorschach, so we took our best guesses.
An artichoke? she laughed, meaning of course
that something of value was hidden from us

under those folds of linen. *A camel?*
she tried again, *No, that vase*
in your parents' bedroom, that awful vase!

and by then I was getting angry, because
all I could pick out was that old
Chevy my friend drove in high school,

the one we'd speed off in after class
let out. *I can't see it,* I said,
Move your leg. She giggled, dragging

the whole mess to the floor with a single
curled toe. She had to be crazy. *Kiss me,*
I said. And she did.

Philip Memmer was born in Ohio, and has lived in Illinois, New Jersey, North Carolina, Oregon, and Pennsylvania. His poems have appeared in *Poetry, Poetry Northwest, Southern Poetry Review, Mid-American Review*, and many other journals and anthologies. He is the also author of two chapbooks of poems, *For Resident* (FootHills Publishing, 2002) and *The Apartment* (piccadilly press, 2001). He now lives in upstate New York, where he edits the poetry journal *Two Rivers Review* and directs the Downtown Writer's Center, the Syracuse affiliate of the YMCA National Writer's Voice.

Printed in the United States
65039LVS00005B/30